VENOR
THE SEA SCORPION

BY ADAM BLADE

ORCHARD

I have waited in the shadows long enough, perfecting myself. Now I will strike at my wretched enemies and make all Nemos bow before me. All I need to complete my plan are the Arms of Addulis: the Spear, the Breastplate, the Sword and the Helmet.

My mother used to tell me stories of their power, and for a long time I thought they were myths. But now I know they are real, buried in this vast ocean and waiting for a new master to wield them. With the Arms of Addulis in my control, no Merryn or human will be able to stop me.

But... I almost hope there is some pathetic hero foolish enough to try. My Robobeasts are ready – unlike anything these oceans have witnessed before. My enemies will learn that their flesh is weak.

Quake before your new leader!

RED EYE

CHAPTER ONE

THE PIRATE HAVEN

Max reached deep into the fuel injection system. Once he had reattached the fuel pump, his modifications to the *Lizard's Revenge* would be finished. "Roger, pass me the turbo wrench," he said.

"Tell me, lad," Roger muttered, as he handed over the wrench with his hooked hand, "why did I let you mess with my ship's engines?"

Ignoring his pirate friend's moans, Max secured the last piece of his turbo-charged pump. "Technically the ship's stolen, so it's not really yours, Roger."

Roger straightened his eye patch. "It's my ship because I liberated it. Law of the sea, crewmate!"

"Hurry up," Lia shouted through a hatch above. "All this messing about has given Siborg a head start!"

"All done!" Max called back. When Lia saw the improvements in action, she'd realise they were worth the delay. They'd more than make up the lost time with the faster engines. How they'd deal with Siborg when they caught up with him was quite another matter, though.

Their mysterious enemy, known as "Red Eye" among the pirates of the Chaos Quadrant, had managed to stay a step ahead at every turn so far. And his last warning had been chilling. He'd hacked Max's dogbot Rivet's circuits and delivered the message that he now considered them "a hostile force", and would destroy them at their next encounter.

Still, Max had to stop Siborg from finding the legendary Arms of Addulis. Max had already defeated Sythid, a giant spider crab with chainsaws on its limbs, to win the Pearl Spear. Then they had fought Brux, a colossal walrus with tusks the size of an aquabike, to keep control of the Stone Breastplate.

Both creatures had been made more terrifying by the addition of advanced technology. Siborg was even better at making hybrids than the Professor was. It was only with the help of Max's friends – Lia, Roger and Grace – and the ancient Merryn battle-gear, that the Robobeasts had been beaten. If Siborg got his hands on the Arms of Addulis, he would wreak havoc above and below water. In short, he would be unstoppable.

"Come on," Lia said. "We've got the Coral

Sword to find."

Max scrambled up the metal rungs onto the ship's bridge, keen to test his improvements. He twisted the ship's starter and the *Lizard's Revenge* roared into life. Lia clamped her webbed hands over her ears. Grinning, Max opened the throttle. The ship leapt forward and water sprayed over the bows as it sliced through the waves.

"We're going thirty per cent faster!" Max yelled. "Siborg won't even see us coming!"

"So, what's so special about this Sword?" asked Roger.

"Legend has it that no material can withstand the edge of its blade," said Lia. "And it gives the bearer incredible speed in attack."

Roger snorted. "Legend has it there's a giant seahorse that lays golden eggs in Zeta Quadrant."

Lia frowned at him.

Max smiled and looked around for Rivet. He could see Roger's niece Grace on deck, fighting a pretend enemy with her plastic cutlass. Rivet was sitting near her with his tongue dangling as sea-spray drenched him. *Back to his normal self*, Max thought happily. He'd been worried after Siborg hacked his dogbot's circuits. "Rivet, come here. Show me the map," Max called.

"Yes, Max." Rivet sprinted onto the bridge. His eyes glowed before projecting a 3-D hologram over the map table. It was an image of the ancient Merryn map that Siborg had stolen. Only two Xs remained – marking the locations of the Coral Sword and the Shell Helmet, the last two of the Arms of Addulis.

Grace charged in from the deck. "Where are we going? I'm ready to fight."

"We're just about to decide." Max pointed toward the mark for the Coral Sword. "Zoom

in, Rivet." The dogbot magnified a small
island shaped like a skull.

"I know that place," Roger said. "Barriosa!"

Lia raised her eyebrows. "Isn't Barriosa a
notorious pirate port?"

"That's right," Roger said. "Had me some
good times there!" He winked at Max.

Roger punched the coordinates into the
navigation system and the ship steered

automatically in the water, the wheel turning of its own accord. Roger turned to Max and Lia, and looked them over. "You'll both need some new clothes, or else you'll stand out like two lobsters in a whiskey glass. Grace and I can fix that."

The delight on Roger's face disturbed Max as they were led into the Captain's Quarters.

"I might not look like a scurvy sea dog, but I itch like one," Max complained, scratching his bandana.

Lia gave him a sympathetic smile, but her blackened teeth made it look gruesome. She wore a long red coat with gaudy gold trim over a bright purple blouse. Max felt just as ridiculous in his ripped blue trousers and ruffled pink shirt. He was hot too – they'd kept their deepsuits on beneath their disguises.

"Approaching Barriosa," Roger called.

Max climbed onto the bridge and checked the control displays. "We got here in less than four hours," he said. "The engines performed better than I imagined."

"Helps to have a good Captain," Roger replied as he steered between two crumbling cliffs. "The entrance to Barriosa."

Roger navigated down the narrow straits into a stinking harbour surrounded by rocky hills. *Only pirates would want to call this place home*, Max thought. Sleek pirate ships painted stealth-black and adorned with skull-and-crossbones flags filled the harbour. The ships bristled with harpoons and cannons. Max checked the weapons console to make sure the *Lizard's Revenge* was ready for any trouble.

As the *Lizard's Revenge* bumped against the long wooden dock that stretched from the town's harbour front, auto-mooring ropes spun out to secure the vessel. Max lowered the gangway onto the quayside. He swallowed nervously. Roger was convinced they could enter pirate territory without causing trouble, but Max wasn't so sure. Where could the Sword possibly be hidden in a place like this?

Grace hurtled up to the bridge with her toy blaster. "Reporting for duty, Uncle, Captain!"

Max strapped on his hyperblade. Barriosa seemed like it could be dangerous.

Roger's one good eye narrowed. "Take that off, landlubber! Barriosa's an old-fashioned sort of place. No fancy weapons here. Your dogbot will be bad luck too."

Max grabbed a cutlass from a weapons locker. He hurried out and down the gangway after Roger, Lia and Grace. Lia stooped at the dock's edge to tell her pet swordfish Spike that they'd be back soon.

"You there," Roger called, flicking a gold doubloon to a sailor. "There'll be another

coin for you to keep my ship safe."

The pirate tugged his cap and took the coin.

Max noticed the knuckles on Lia's webbed fingers were white as she adjusted the straps on her Amphibio mask. *We're both fish out of water here*, Max realised.

Grace charged ahead down the quayside, leading them to the row of dingy taverns lining the docks. The taverns' names were scrawled on pieces of shipwrecks nailed above the doors: *The Keelhauled Pirate's Purse, The Whole Lobster Trouble, The Yardarm Jigger.* The sound of arguing, fighting and bad singing spilled out into the street. Roger looked longingly at the tavern entrances, but Max grabbed his arm and steered him away. "We've more important things to do, Roger."

"Shame," he replied glumly. "Come on, the coordinates for the Sword are this way."

A one-legged beggar hobbled on his crutches to block their path. Around his neck hung a fiddle cobbled together from sardine cans and fish guts.

"Coin for a song?" he shouted as he started to play. It sounded worse to Max than the Merryn gill-warbling opera Lia's dad was always playing in the royal palace.

"Blistering typhoons," Roger snapped. "Out

of our way!"

The beggar limped aside, muttering about manners, but Max felt him watching as they marched away from the water's edge. The streets were getting narrower and the shadows in the doorways growing darker.

Max checked their position on his GPS watch. They were close to the Coral Sword's coordinates. "We need to take the next left."

As they turned the corner, Roger's face lit up at the sight of a weathered tavern called *Old Cap'n Grant's*. "If you and Lia can look after Grace, I'll make some enquiries inside."

Lia frowned. "Wait a second, Roger. Why is the Sword of Addulis in a tavern?"

"Maybe it was buried here before Barriosa became a port?" Max suggested.

"Shiver me timbers, he's not giving up!" Roger cursed, glancing back at the top of the alley. As the one-legged beggar rode his crutches full steam towards them, Roger pulled another gold coin from his pocket. He tossed it towards the beggar. "Sling your hook. You'll not get another penny from me."

The beggar made no attempt even to catch the coin. The hairs on the back of Max's neck stood up. *Something is wrong*, he realised, pulling out his cutlass.

A pirate jumped from a doorway and snatched Grace up. She kicked and screamed, "Leave us alone! We're pirates!"

"You're no pirates." The beggar unfolded his missing leg and let his crutches clatter to the floor. "Siborg be expecting yar," he said with a toothless grin. He pulled a blade from behind his back as more pirates appeared around them. "There's no escape, not if you want your little friend to live."

Max dropped his sword.

This Quest just got a lot more deadly.

CHAPTER TWO

A GUNPOWDER PLOT

"Get below, you lousy dogs," the beggar ordered, pointing at the steps outside *Old Cap'n Grant's*.

Grace kicked against the pirate holding her. "Let me go!"

"Save it," snapped the pirate and carried her down the rough stone steps.

Max followed them into a dank cellar. Stinking torches flickered, casting shadows behind the barrels of rum and wooden crates.

The beggar shoved Max and his friends into a storage room and slammed the door. There was a rattle as a thick chain was secured around the door. "You can rot in there until Siborg comes," the beggar yelled.

"I see why they'd be suspicious of you two," Roger muttered. "But I'm as salty and scurvy as they come!"

Lia rolled her eyes. "How did Siborg get one step ahead of us again?"

"We'll figure that out later," Max said. "We need to escape first." He tore off his bandana. "No need to keep up the pretence now!"

They all stripped down to their deepsuits, then Max and Roger dragged the barrels aside, in case there was a hatch or drain in the floor. Nothing. The walls were solid stone without any windows. Above them, through the wooden floor, they could hear the singing from the tavern full of bloodthirsty pirates.

"At least we won't starve." Roger grinned as he cracked open a crate labelled *Ship's Grub*. He scooped out a handful of golden snacks and offered them around.

"What are they?" Max asked.

"The finest chilli-salted starfish legs this side of the Chaos Quadrant."

Max reached out for one, but Lia shot him

a look. The Merryn didn't agree with eating sea creatures. If he ate a starfish leg, he'd never hear the end of it. "I'll pass, thanks, Roger."

"Suit yourself, more for me!" Roger crunched on a starfish leg, but quickly started choking. He clutched his throat. "Hot, hot – aargh!"

Lia grinned as Roger panicked. He picked up a small flask, pulled out the stopper with his teeth, and took a swig. He spat out a plume of black powder. "The rum's dried out."

"I'm not so sure." Max examined the powder. "This is our way out, Roger – gunpowder! Find something to light it with."

As Roger and Grace searched the room, Max got out his fetchpad. He had a plan, and set about reprogramming the gadget.

Lia frowned as he worked. "Doesn't your fetchpad summon your hydrodisk?"

"Not any more," Max replied, tipping over a barrel. "Help me get as much of this powder under the door as possible."

"Ha, found something!" Roger held up an electro-flint and a fuse. "We'll show those landlubbers who the *real* pirates are!"

"Everyone get back!" Max ordered. He lit the fuse and sheltered behind the barrels with the others. He plugged his fingers into his ears and closed his eyes.

The explosion rocked the room, showering Max with splinters of wood. He shook off the debris and peered over the top of the barrels. As the smoke cleared, he saw that the door was completely gone.

Boots thundered across the wooden ceiling above, followed by confused shouts.

"We're under attack!"

"Don't let Siborg down!"

"Get them prisoners before they be escaping!"

An ash-covered pirate staggered in with a pair of cutlasses in his hands. "What in the seven seas is goin' on?" he cried.

Max crouched as he heard metallic feet clattering down the stone stairs. Then Rivet bounded in and knocked the pirate to the floor with a single leap.

"Coming, Max!" Rivet's tail thumped down on the fallen sailor's head.

"Good boy!" said Max. "I programmed the fetchpad to bring Rivet," he added, turning to the others.

"Time we made ourselves scarce," Roger muttered, snatching up the fallen pirate's cutlass and pulling Grace with him. Max and Lia scrambled after him. In the corner of the cellar, a pirate from the tavern appeared – and then another. They opened fire with their blasters and the stonework above Max's head exploded.

He ducked and ran after Lia, Roger and Grace up the steps into the alleyway outside.

"This way," hissed Roger.

They plunged through the streets towards the docks. Max glanced back and saw Lia struggling to keep up with him. Merryn were as fast as seals in the water, but her Aqua Powers didn't help on land.

"Save yourself," she yelled.

Max couldn't leave her behind. If Lia couldn't go any faster, he needed to slow down the pirates. He spied a washing line criss-crossing above the lane. It sagged under the weight of fancy shirts, brightly coloured waistcoats and skull-and-crossbones flags. Max took a running leap for the sign outside the *Long Tom Silver* tavern. He swung himself up and snapped the washing line.

Clothes rained down on the pirates, tripping them up. Max grabbed Lia's hand and helped her onto Rivet's back. "Hold on tight!" he said, then patted Rivet on the rump. "Run, boy!"

The dogbot took off at speed with Lia clinging to his back, and Max ran behind them through the winding streets. Just as he was beginning to think they were lost, they emerged back at the harbour front.

Roger and Grace were already on the jetty and leapt aboard the ship. Roger dived for the bridge and the ship's engines growled into life. As Max and Rivet jumped off the dockside as well, Roger shouted, "Untie the moorings!"

Lia scrambled off the dogbot and whistled for Spike. The swordfish leapt from the water and slashed the mooring ropes clear. The sea churned up around them as Roger threw the throttle into reverse.

All along the dockside, robotic arms sprang up from the iron mooring posts. Cannons swivelled around to face the *Lizard's Revenge* and fired. A huge fountain of water exploded close by. "All hands on deck," Roger yelled.

"Let's be sailing faster than an octopus in a twister!"

The *Lizard's Revenge* roared out of Barriosa as laser fire erupted from the shore. *So much for low-tech*, thought Max. Laser beams zapped the ship's toughened alloy hull. Roger swerved the ship out of the harbour and down the

strait into the open sea. Max watched behind them, but there was no sign of pursuit.

Grace waved her plastic blaster as she whooped. "We escaped!"

Max checked the sonar. Nothing was chasing them out of Barriosa. *It doesn't make sense*, he thought. *Why just let us go? Unless…*

He scanned the sea ahead of them. *Something* was emerging from the bubbling surface of the ocean. Max checked the sonar again and his heart hammered somewhere up in his throat. A giant spherical ship, almost too big for the sonar screen, was rising from the ocean floor on six long tapered legs. The sea boiled and bubbled. The ship broke the surface and hundreds of domed portholes stared out like spiders' eyes.

Max felt the blood rush from his face. "What is that thing?" he whispered.

The loudspeaker crackled. "This is my lab-ship," said a clinical voice. "I call her the *Hive*."

It's Siborg! Max swallowed his fear. "What have you done with the Coral Sword?" he demanded.

"You know, I'm very disappointed," replied the voice. "I expected more from the famous Max and Lia." Laughter crackled over the radio. "You really thought an artefact of such importance was in a pirate tavern? I changed the map in your dogbot's memory drive." Siborg tutted. "Such a basic trick. While you walked into my trap I recovered the Sword from its real resting place."

"Prove it," Max said. "Show yourself and the Sword!"

"I'd rather you surrendered and gave me the other weapons," Siborg replied. "Before I destroy your pathetic vessel."

"I'll give him pathetic," Roger muttered. "The *Lizard's Revenge* is top of the range! I'd

rather die than surrender!"

"I thought you might be that stupid," Siborg
sighed. "Very well."

A large hatch on Siborg's lab-ship scraped
open. Max gripped his hyperblade and gazed
in horror as two ten-foot long claws emerged,
followed by a body half the size of the *Lizard's
Revenge*, covered in an armoured exoskeleton.
The creature darted forward on eight clawed

legs. A thick muscular tail curled up to reveal a mechanical black stinger at its tip, with tanks of green venom.

Siborg's created a monster sea scorpion!

The scorpion swivelled its yellow eyes towards Roger's ship and bared a mouth full of razor-sharp teeth. Max's heart was pounding and his body felt numb.

"Meet Venor," Siborg said.

CHAPTER THREE

TEN MINUTES TO SURRENDER

Venor's eyes fixed on the *Lizard's Revenge* before it launched into the water. Jets erupted from its sides, propelling it forward.

"Open fire, me hearties!" Roger yelled.

Max ran for the weapon controls, activating the forward blaster cannons. A targeting screen lit up. Using the joystick controller, he lined up the scorpion in his sights and fired all three cannons. Venor swerved, dodging the deathly blasts. It flexed his armoured body and dived under the water.

"It's Davy Jones's Locker for us, if we're not careful," Roger shouted. "Grace, deploy the depth charges."

"Take that, you nasty bug!" Grace shouted, slamming the firing mechanism.

A dozen depth charges were catapulted from the bow of the ship. Max tracked them on the sonar as they plunged towards Venor. Roger swung the *Lizard's Revenge* away from the kill zone. An explosion sent a great spout of water from the surface, rocking the ship. Venor was blown sideways, but within seconds he surged towards the ship again.

"His circuits must be blast-resistant," Max gasped.

"He's too fast to outrun," Roger moaned.

"I've got an idea," Lia said. She ran to the lockers at the back of the bridge, opened one, and grabbed the Pearl Spear of Addulis.

"Lia, wait," Max said, but Lia shook her head and leapt into the water.

Max hoped she knew what she was doing. He watched on the sonar as she and Spike raced towards the scorpion. Venor stabbed out with its stinger, forcing Lia to somersault away from Spike. She used the spear to block a deadly claw, and then dodged aside with a nimble twitch of her webbed feet. Despite her thrusts with the ancient Merryn weapon, Lia wasn't even able to make contact with Venor. Spike swam in to pull her away, but the creature's claw struck again, sending them both spinning into the ocean.

"No!" Max yelled. He fired torpedoes at the creature. They exploded against the shielded Robobeast, knocking it back. Venor turned and sped through the waters towards the *Lizard's Revenge*. Its legs clanged against the hull as the creature tore off a sheet of alloy plating and tossed it into the sea. The sea scorpion scrambled up the starboard side, its weight rocking the ship.

"Max!" Roger yelled. "Stop that thing before it eats my ship!"

"Leave it to me," Max said. He accessed the ship's electric circuits. If blasting the

Robobeast didn't work, perhaps frying it would. "Stand clear," he shouted as he redirected the ship's power to the alloy hull, sending every volt of power the engines had into the scorpion.

Blue sparks crackled in arcs across the ship towards Venor. Dazzling lightning exploded around the Robobeast. As the blur of light in Max's eyes cleared, Venor leapt forward, ripping more bits off the vessel. Green venom pulsed from its stinger, burning like acid where it splashed on the hull. *It's really mad now*, Max thought.

Siborg radioed again. "You have ten minutes to surrender," he said, "or Venor will kill you all."

The scorpion dropped what was left of a gun turret before digging its razor-sharp legs into the hull. It stopped moving and its yellow eyes glared at the bridge.

Roger cleared his throat. "Well, crewmate, Grace and I might go and liberate ourselves another ship before that monster starts looking for dessert."

"You won't get far, Venor's too fast," Lia said, staggering back onto the bridge with the Pearl Spear.

Max was glad she had made it back to the ship. "Lia's right, we can't run and we can't give up. If Siborg uses the Arms of Addulis alongside his advanced technology, nowhere on Nemos will be safe!"

He closed his eyes, and tried to think clearly. But with an angry Robobeast squatting just a few feet away, it was hard.

"Venor must have a weakness," muttered Lia. Max's eyes flicked open. That was it!

"I know what would make us faster than Venor," Max said. "The Sword of Addulis!"

Lia rolled her eyes. "Yes, but Siborg has the

Coral Sword."

Max grinned. "Then he won't expect us to sneak on board his ship to get it."

A gold tooth flashed in Roger's smile. "We'll make a pirate out of you yet," he said, then shook his head. "But Siborg is watching the *Lizard's Revenge*. As soon as we step off the ship, Venor is going to come after us."

"Nine minutes," Siborg announced over the radio.

"What if we wear disguises?" Grace said. "Then he won't see us!"

Max realised that Grace was on to something. "If we jettison the ship's waste fuel it will hide us from his sensors."

"Best use the emergency escape hatches." Roger fiddled with the control systems, then pressed a large red shiny button on his captain's chair. The navigation control panel slid forward and shot up on hydraulic arms to reveal a row of escape tubes. Grace strapped on a breathing mask and jumped into a tube.

"Hold on, Grace," Roger said. "You're not going with them!"

"But I'll be safer out there than I will be on the ship," she replied.

Roger sighed. "That's me girl, but if things look dangerous, you swim like lightning!"

"Aren't you coming with us, Roger?" Max asked in surprise.

"A captain can't abandon his ship," Roger replied, a crack in his voice. "Now get going!"

Max wondered if that was the real reason. Roger rarely did anything courageous, but it made sense for someone to stay behind on the ship. Max, Lia and Rivet sprinted for the escape tubes. Max slipped into the small metallic chamber and crouched down. "Seal me up, Roger," he called.

"Good luck, crewmates," Roger said. "I'll activate the waste fuel pumps once you're away. That should give you plenty of cover."

With a hiss, a metal hatch clamped down over the top of Max's escape tube.

Water flooded the tube. The chamber floor slid away and Max was fired into the sea.

We're coming for you, Siborg!

CHAPTER FOUR

AN EVIL GENIUS

Max plunged through the dark, oily water, holding his breath so he didn't have to taste the fuel through his gills. He kicked forward, trying to find the others in the murky water.

There wasn't a moment to lose.

He saw Lia shoot downwards on Spike with Grace clinging to her back as he and Rivet cleared the polluted water. Lia's silver hair streamed behind her and Grace's breathing mask left a trail of bubbles.

"Faster, Rivet." *No sign that Siborg's seen us yet…*

Max caught up with Lia near the base of the lab-ship.

"How are we going to get in?" she asked.

"We need to find some sort of service hatch," Max said.

"Like that one?" Grace pointed to a circular door just above the surface.

"Perfect!" Max said. "Rivet, tread water. And Spike, you wait here for us."

He climbed onto the dogbot's back and scrambled up onto a ledge in front of the hatch. He readied his hyperblade then turned a wheel to unlock the door. The hatch swung open without alarms sounding.

That's the first bit of luck we've had in a long while, Max thought.

As Rivet clawed inside with Grace on his back and Lia behind him, Max activated the

dogbot's searchlights. Two beams of light burst from Rivet's eyes. Thick bundles of cable dangling from the ceiling cast eerie shadows down the curved corridor. "This way!" said Max, nerves tingling.

He led them inside Siborg's ship. Cables brushed against his head and it was so cold that he could see his breath turn to mist.

The corridor was blocked by two massive metal doors painted with the large red-eye emblem of Siborg. Next to the doorway was a weird three-fingered recognition pad. Max squeezed his fingers into the slots, but nothing happened. He tried pushing the door but it was locked firm.

"Dead end," Max said. "We're wasting time without a map. Rivet, make a 3-D scan of the vessel."

"Yes, Max!" Rivet shuffled around in a tight circle, raising and dropping his head as though he had learnt some strange pirate jig from Roger. Finally, the searchlights from Rivet's eyes dimmed, plunging them into darkness before a hologram of the *Hive* appeared.

The ship's corridors were arranged in ever tightening circles around a massive central chamber. It reminded Max of the cross-section of a conch shell, except it had as many levels as it did twisting corridors.

Lia gasped. "This is a symbol sacred to the Merryn. Why would a pirate use it to build a ship?"

Max shrugged. "Must be a coincidence!"

I need a closer look at how the vessel works.

He yanked a cluster of cables away from a wall panel and prised it open with the tip of his hyperblade. A colourful array of fine transparent tubes lined the walls behind the panel. Blue and red liquids raced through the tubes like blood,with hundreds of tiny bubbles being swept along with them. The ship was using a truly advanced power source.

"This is revolutionary," Max explained to Lia and Grace. "The ship isn't powered by the combustion of regular fuel. If I'm right, these tubes help split particles of water themselves at a molecular level."

Lia stared blankly at him. Max wished technology interested her. "Honestly," he said. "It's incredible! Whoever built this was a genius. Way cleverer than the Professor."

Lia narrowed her eyes and made a noise of disapproval at that.

"A twisted evil genius, of course," Max corrected as he studied the hologram again. "Anyway, that large chamber at the centre of the lab-ship looks a good place to keep a sword safe."

Max led them down another corridor, but they were stopped again by a locked doorway with the same weird three-finger sensor.

"We have to work out how to bypass these security doors," Max said, breaking open the panel. Muffled clunks and hisses echoed down the corridor.

"What's that noise?" Grace asked.

Rivet's ears pricked up and he ran off. Max, Lia and Grace chased after the dogbot.

They found him sniffing at another door. To Max's surprise, the door hissed open and the thrum of machinery and clanking got louder.

Max rubbed Rivet's head. "Good boy,"

he said. "His internal signals must have somehow tricked the door into opening."

Grace darted between them, pointing her plastic blaster. "Attack!"

"Wait!" Max chased after her with his hyperblade. "We don't know what's in there."

Grace had stopped just inside the room, her jaw hanging open. Conveyor belts zigzagged across the room ferrying parts between machines. Presses and rollers flattened metal into sheets before stamps pressed out parts to be welded together. Pincers shuttled newly made parts overhead toward assembling machines.

"There's nobody here," Lia said.

"It's fully automatic." Max approached the nearest conveyor belt and picked up what looked like a heavy-duty foot with three long metallic toes. He replaced it on the conveyor.

"What's it for?" Lia asked.

Pincers shot down from above and whisked the foot to another machine that attached the foot to a leg assembly. It plunked the leg down on another belt where motors and cables were soldered onto it. Above, robot torsos zipped past on hooks suspended from the ceiling towards another conveyor belt, this time covered in heads.

Max ran over and picked one up. "This factory is making cyrates!" he gasped.

"It's creepy," Grace said, biting her lip.

Max examined the cyrate head more carefully. "Siborg must be improving his design. He's making these ones out of an advanced polymer instead of metal."

"But why?" Lia asked.

"To make them harder to defeat," said Max. "He's learning."

There was a hiss as two doors opened around a large central chamber. Glistening, oily body parts were shunted out as more parts zoomed in. From the markings on the chamber, Max knew this was where high-powered sprays coated the robot parts with a protective chemical layer. He wrinkled his nose. It was nasty stuff.

With her plastic blaster, Grace poked at a cyrate torso. "You don't scare me."

Pincers dropped down, grabbing the torso. Grace screamed as the pincer snagged her sleeve too and hoisted her up into the air. Max tried to grab her, but it was too late. He watched in horror as the little girl was whisked off, deeper into the factory.

CHAPTER FIVE

BATTLE SUIT

"Get off me!" Grace screamed, dangling from the pincer.

It swept her away over the conveyor belts criss-crossing the factory.

"I'm coming!" Max yelled.

He scaled the nearest conveyor belt, scattering cyrate heads with his feet. He chased after her, ducking a line of robotic legs whizzing past. He leapt from one conveyor belt to another, climbing higher and higher as Grace zoomed ahead of him, wailing and thrashing. He grabbed a cyrate arm dangling from the assembly line and swung out to catch the bottom of Grace's trousers, but she was still out of reach. He glanced ahead and swallowed. His friend was being taken to the chemical coating chamber. If he didn't stop her, she'd be suffocated by the deadly fumes!

He spotted a crane arm suspended high above the factory floor. It was his only hope. He leapt over to the scaffolding and scrambled up, then edged along the arm. It began to sink with his weight. He shinned faster and, just as Grace passed underneath him, Max struck out with his hyperblade, slicing her free of the pincers.

Grace dropped onto the assembly line below, scattering cyrate parts everywhere. She looked a little dazed, but punched the air. "That's what I call an adventure!"

Max swung down to join her and Lia. His headset buzzed and he activated it.

"Max, six minutes until I'm scorpion food!" Roger told him.

"We're working as fast as we can," Max replied. "Over and out." He turned to the others. "This ship's huge and we've only managed to open one door so far."

"I've had a thought about that," Lia said. She scooped up a half-assembled arm from the floor and ran over to the nearest door. She pressed the three-fingered robotic hand into the security slot and with a whoosh, the door slid open.

Clever! A cyrate hand for a cyrate security print, Max thought. "You're getting as good at technology as me!"

Lia grinned, but then her smile fell away and she sucked in a gasp.

Max hurried over to see what had disturbed the Merryn princess and skidded to a halt at the threshold. Inside the next chamber were row upon row of assembled cyrates with slumped shoulders, painted black and emblazoned with a red eye. Deadly-looking blasters poked up over their bowed heads. Hyperblades were strapped to their hips. Looking around, Max counted over a hundred rows of battle-ready cyrates.

"Are they sleeping?" Grace asked.

Max nodded. "I don't think they've been activated yet," he whispered. "But let's not hang around, just in case."

They hurried past the skeletal robots. Across from the cyrate army were a series of dark holes in the floor. Max carefully peered down into the chutes. They were just like the escape tubes on the *Lizard's Revenge*.

"I bet these tubes blast the cyrates outside the ship like torpedoes," he said.

"Now's not the time for sightseeing," Lia hissed. "My Aqua Powers are making my head throb. We must be getting closer to the Coral Sword."

They headed for an alcove on the furthest side of the huge room. Large screens and control panels filled the walls. Cyrate icons on the screens showed all the battle droids labelled as "inactive".

"This must be the central command function for the cyrates," Max said.

Lia leant against the control panel and clutched her temples. "It's here somewhere," she said, frowning. Then she looked up and pointed to a hatch in the ceiling. "Up there!"

"I bet this button has something to do with it!" Grace said as she raced towards a black switch on the floor.

Max grabbed her. "Wait, it might be another trap. Rivet, press the button and come back."

Rivet leapt onto the button then scrambled to Max's side. "Done, Max!"

A transparent tube slid down from the ceiling with a hiss. It landed with a thud. Inside was a robot three times as big as Max. It had long arms that hung down to its knees and a large viewing panel in its chest. It bristled with weapons on every limb, from rockets and blasters on its legs to laser rifles on its arms. One hand clutched a flame-red sword. "The Sword of Addulis," Lia gasped.

Max stared at the weapon. It looked beautiful and deadly at the same time. Its handle was made from a dark scarlet piece of polished coral and its double-edged blade

ended in a slender tip. The tube retracted, leaving the robot behind. Max gripped the hilt of his hyperblade, expecting an attack, but the robot slumped slightly without the support of the tube. Perhaps it wasn't a robot at all. It looked like a sophisticated version of the exo-suits the Aquoran dockworkers used to help them lift heavy objects.

"Unless I'm mistaken, this is Siborg's battle suit," Max said.

"Max!" Roger's voice crackled from his headset. "Four minutes remaining!"

Grace grabbed the sword and tried to twist it free. "It won't budge."

Lia helped her tug, pull and wriggle the sword. She shot Max a look of exasperation. "Don't just stand there, help us!"

Max tried to prise open the robot's fingers, but the hand was locked solid. He pressed his hyperblade against the metal tendons on the back of the hand and sliced them apart. Coils of metal sprang out as the hand released the sword. He grabbed it before it hit the floor.

"Told you we'd get it!" Max grinned, holding it up.

A second later, loud sirens sounded on both sides of the massive room. "Intruder alert! Intruder alert!"

Max passed the Coral Sword to Lia. "Let's get out of here."

Max darted out of the control room with Lia, Grace and Rivet behind him. He hadn't taken more than a couple of steps before every cyrate in the room raised its head. He stopped. Hundreds of glowing red eyes swivelled to face them as the front row of cyrates drew their hyperblade cutlasses.

Grace raised her toy blaster, but Max stood before her, trying to stop his knees trembling.

He was about to face Siborg's entire army.

CHAPTER SIX

DEADLY SWORDS

A line of twenty cyrates formed a wall of death with their swishing hyperblades. Max, Lia and Rivet would have to go through them in order to escape the room. Lia pulled Max back.

"Let me deal with this," she said, holding up the Coral Sword. Before Max could stop her, she charged at the cyrates.

Lia and the Merryn sword glowed with blue iridescence as Addulis's ancient power flowed around them. She severed the arms of the first two cyrates she encountered before somersaulting in a blur of speed.

Lia was right about the Sword's power!

Blades flashed around Lia, but none was quick enough to catch her. With a sweeping slice, she chopped the heads off several

robots before cutting the legs from under another. The last cyrate in the line to hit the deck cleaved neatly in half as if it was a seaweed cake. Lia flicked back her silver hair.

Her victory was short-lived. Another row of cyrates stepped forward, pulling blasters from their backs. The hum of thirty state-of-the-art weapons charging up made Max's stomach tighten with dread. He yanked Grace and Lia to the floor just as blaster fire sizzled overhead and exploded against the walls.

"There's too many to defeat!" he yelled. "We've got to force our way out of here. Follow me and Rivet."

Rivet charged the line. He knocked cyrates aside like an aquabowl ball. Max chased after him with Grace, letting Lia bring up the rear with the ancient weapon. Max ducked under a cyrate's sword. He felt the blade catch his hair but he kept going. He dodged and kicked away the metal claws trying to grab him and Grace.

"Head for the door!" he told Roger's niece.

Movement flashed in the corner of his eye and he flipped backwards as a cyrate's hyperblade swished past his head.

Max launched himself at the robot. The cyrate parried his slash and then dodged as he lunged for its legs. Every move he made was countered by the robot. *It knows how I fight*, Max realised. Siborg must have developed new programming.

As he blocked another chop, something bounced off the cyrate's head. Max glanced around and saw Grace bob up behind an assembly line and throw a cyrate ankle joint at the two robots attacking Lia. *It's time to end this*, Max decided.

He ducked a sideswipe from the cyrate

and then pretended to back away. The robot lurched after him, but Max sprang forward, driving his hyperblade through its chest. Sparks burst from the cyrate as it collapsed. Max grabbed its blaster and fired at Lia's attackers. He blasted one of them apart and, in a blur of action, the Merryn princess finished off another, slicing off both arms and head.

More were coming. Relentlessly.

Rivet broke through and Max sprinted after him into the factory room, snatching up Grace on the way.

"Come on!" he yelled to Lia.

She dashed away from the remaining cyrates and dived through the doorway. Max slammed a spare cyrate arm into the control panel and the door crashed shut. Max quickly hit the panel with his hyperblade, obliterating it in an explosion of sparks. *That should mess the circuits up nicely.*

"That was close!" he said.

Before Lia could reply, Siborg's voice crackled from the ship's speaker system. "It's been entertaining. You've put up a good fight, but when I override the door circuits, you'll be facing hundreds of cyrates. Each one has been programmed to defeat your best fighting techniques. I estimate your chances of survival to be 0.4%." Siborg paused. "It's time to surrender."

Max looked at Lia and Grace. They were dripping with sweat, but they both shook their heads. Max took a deep breath and squared his chest. "No one is going to surrender, except for you, Siborg!"

"Prepare to die, then," Siborg replied.

Max eyed the door nervously and wondered how long he, Lia and Grace could hold off Siborg's army. *What we need is a way to disable all the cyrates at once*, he thought. He huddled closer to Lia and Grace and hoped that Siborg couldn't hear him.

"It's our only chance," Max explained. "We have to return to the control area. It's their weakest spot. Destroy those computers and Siborg can't control the cyrates."

Lia handed him the Coral Sword. "You'll need this," she said. "May the luck of the Merryn be with you. I'll keep Grace safe."

The door groaned, and opened a fraction. Several cyrate claws reached through the gap. Max swung onto the back of Rivet. He held out the Sword of Addulis as though he were an ancient Merryn knight riding a swordfish.

The cyrates slid the door open, massing for attack. Max dug his heels into Rivet. "Charge!"

The dogbot galloped bravely towards the doorway and Max swung the Coral

Sword at the cyrates. In a blur of sparks and severed robotic limbs, he smashed into the battle line. "Keep going, Rivet," he yelled, struggling to hang on. The dogbot bashed his way forward. He stomped cyrates down with his front paws and kicked them away with his back legs. Max wheeled the sword at the attacking cyrates, but they were pressing closer all the time, their claws tearing at his deepsuit.

"Riv, forward flip!" shouted Max.

Rivet stopped dead, front legs clamping onto the floor as his hindquarters jerked upwards, throwing Max into the air above the cyrates. Blaster fire zipped past him and exploded against the ceiling. As he landed, he rolled and sprinted the remaining distance to the control area. He raised the Sword of Addulis and thrust it deep into the control panel. Sparks exploded from the machinery

and alarms shrieked.

Max glanced across the battle room. Cyrates were stamping towards him.

"This has to work," he muttered as he ground the blade back and forth in the console. The panel crackled and fizzed, but the cyrates kept coming. *Perhaps I was wrong.*

Maybe they're controlled from somewhere else!

He looked up to see a cyrate striding towards him, cutlass at the ready. Max twisted the ancient Merryn weapon one last time before ripping it out of the machine to fight.

Abruptly, the cyrate stopped.

They all did, shoulders drooping, cutlasses and blasters dropping from their claw-hands to the ground.

"You did it!" called Lia from across the room.

"Very clever," Siborg's voice boomed. "But in two minutes, Venor will chew up your ship and spit her out."

Max's gaze fell on the launch tubes he'd spotted earlier. "It's the only way to get back to Roger before the scorpion destroys the *Lizard's Revenge*," he said, pointing at them.

"Last one out is a rotten Robobeast," Grace

yelled as she sprinted for the launch tubes, strapping on her breathing mask before vanishing from sight. "Woohoo!"

Max nodded to Lia. It was now or never.

CHAPTER SEVEN

TIME RUNS OUT

Max gripped the Coral Sword tight as he jumped feet first into the launch tube. Jets of air blasted him through the long metal tube. He ricocheted into a bend, his eyes watering. Suddenly, Max's stomach lurched as the tube plummeted downwards.

He slammed out of the tube into the sea like a missile, plunging into a confusion of bubbles and currents. He kicked up, fighting against the force pulling him down. He spotted Grace swimming away from the

Hive. Spike swam for Lia as Rivet arrived at Max's side.

"Play again, Max," he barked.

"Later, Riv," he replied. "We need to get back to the ship to save Roger."

In less than a minute, Venor would finish ripping the *Lizard's Revenge* apart. Max swam for the ship. Fuel was pooling around the hull and pieces of panelling bobbed in the water. He didn't know how much more the ship could take.

"Max!" Grace screamed.

Max spun around. Two cyrates were blasting through the water towards her. Lia and Spike surged towards one, narrowly dodging the robot's hyperblade. Spike twisted around faster than the robot could and impaled the cyrate on his sword. The robot's body jerked a few times, then it slid off the sword and sank to the bottom of the ocean.

The other cyrate grabbed Grace around the waist. "Let me go, you bucket of sardines," she screamed. It was trying to drag her back to the *Hive*, despite her best efforts to kick and punch the robot.

"Rivet, attack!" Max yelled. He launched himself through the water towards Grace.

Rivet powered past Max, his propellers working overtime. Before Max had halved the distance to the cyrate, the dogbot had his jaws crunched around the robot's leg. The cyrate tried to shake off the growling fishing droid, but his bite was too strong.

The cyrate's grip on Grace slipped and she pulled away. The robot grabbed Grace's breathing mask and yanked it off as Rivet tore the robot's leg away, trailing wires. With only a single leg-thruster working, the one-legged cyrate started to spin in circles.

Max would have chased it, but without her breathing mask Grace would drown. He slipped the sword into his belt next to his hyperblade and grabbed her waist. With his other hand he held Rivet's collar. "Up, boy – quick!"

Water streamed around Max as Rivet propelled him and Grace rapidly to the surface of the water. They burst out into the fresh air close to Lia and Spike.

Grace took a big gulp of air and heaved up sea water. "Did you see me wrestle that cyrate?" she asked, wiping her mouth.

Max scanned the *Lizard's Revenge*. The Robobeast was facing away from them, its armoured tail flexing menacingly. "We need to sneak back aboard," Max said. "Rivet, you'll be too loud climbing the hull. Go to the cargo bay and meet us on the bridge."

"Yes, Max," Rivet replied, then dived.

Max struck out for the iron ladder on the side of the ship. He clambered up slowly, trying not to alert the scorpion. When he reached the top, he beckoned Lia and Grace to follow him. He watched Venor. "Head for the bridge, I'll cover you," he said.

As Max's friends ran off, Siborg's voice boomed from the speakers on the scorpion's body. "Your ten minutes are up."

Venor bellowed. It dug its claws into the ship's hull. It ripped off a communication dish and hurtled it across the ship to where Lia and Grace were heading.

"Watch out!" Max yelled.

The girls ducked before it hit them, but Venor twisted around. It glared at Max and its jaws twitched hungrily. The Robobeast stamped towards him, causing the ship to sway violently. Max used the Coral Sword to keep his balance. "Keep going!" he yelled to Lia and Grace.

Max edged forward. The scorpion's legs would be its weakest point: he'd strike there. But Venor's weight shifted again, rocking the ship unexpectedly. The deck slipped from under Max's feet and he hit it hard. Winded, he started sliding toward the Robobeast's open mouth. Its thin, razor-sharp teeth glistened with toxic saliva. The terrible scorpion was

going to eat him alive!

Max stabbed the Coral Sword into the deck to stop his slide. Venor hissed and stalked towards him with its tail raised, ready to strike. Max scrambled back, desperate to escape the scorpion bearing down on him.

Roger burst from the bridge armed with

the biggest blaster that Max had ever seen. It was a top-of-the-line disruptor ray. "Time to walk the plank, you overgrown bug!" Roger yelled.

He fired a salvo of pulses at Venor. They crackled against the Robobeast's armour. Venor roared with anger. It lashed out at Roger, knocking the blaster out of the pirate's

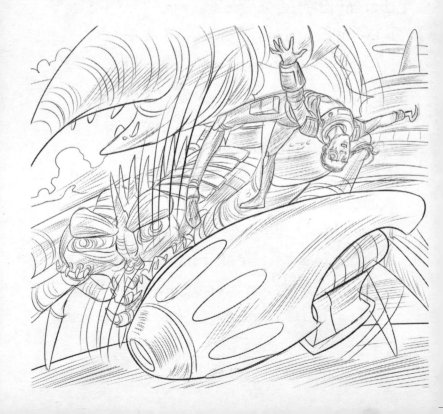

hands as he slammed into the deck on his back. The scorpion reared over him.

"It's time you learned that no one defies me," Siborg boomed.

Venor's giant stinger pulsed with a vile green liquid. It lifted its muscular tail up menacingly in the air.

Then the scorpion's sting slammed into the middle of Roger's chest. The pirate's body twitched and stilled.

"No!" Max yelled, falling to his knees.

CHAPTER EIGHT

A WATERY GRAVE

Max stared around for help and saw Grace's head poking out of the hatch to the bridge. Her eyes were full of confusion and fear. He didn't know what he could say to her to make it better. Anger burned in Max's chest. Roger might have lived on the wrong side of the law, but he was still a friend and had a good heart. They'd come such a long way together since they had met saving the Sea Ghosts from the Professor.

Venor pulled back his stinger, flicking Roger's limp body into the water.

Max stood up and pulled the Coral Sword from the deck. He couldn't let his emotions get in his way. There would be time to mourn Roger, but first he needed to defeat Venor. Lia and Grace emerged from the bridge, wiping tears from their eyes. Max turned from them and glared at Venor.

"Siborg, you'll pay for this!" he yelled.

He threw the Coral Sword to Lia. "Keep Grace safe," he said and slid out his hyperblade. "It's time I dealt with Venor once and for all!"

Max scooped up Roger's blaster. With his hyperblade in one hand and the blaster in the other, Max faced the scorpion. Venor sneered at him and flexed its claws. More green venom pulsed to the end of its tail.

"You're courageous, Max," Siborg called

from Venor's speakers. "Even though you
have the Professor's blood inside you. It's a
shame I have no choice but to kill you."

Max gripped the hyperblade and blaster
tighter. Siborg's words struck him as odd.

How does he know about my connection with the Professor? Max thought. *Could he be from Aquora too?*

Max didn't have time to think about it. Venor lurched at him with its claws. Max ducked out of the way and fired the blaster at the scorpion's luminous yellow eyes.

There must be a central processing unit somewhere on the Robobeast's body, he thought. *Destroy it and I sever Siborg's link to his creation.*

Max targeted the scorpion's face again, but each blast only enraged the Robobeast further. The scorpion jabbed at him with its sting as well.

Max parried the scorpion's claws with his hyperblade. Venor stabbed again, this time with its front feet. As the legs smashed down towards him, Max rolled and slid underneath the scorpion's plated body. The insect's armour glistened with a metallic film.

It's got the same protective coating as the new cyrates!

Max stared up at the scorpion's underbelly. Venor's claws were busy ripping up the deck. It hurled pieces towards the bridge where Lia and Grace were sheltering. Max needed to do something fast before the creature forced his friends into the open.

He slashed at the scorpion's leg, hoping its armour would be vulnerable to his hyperblade. Sparks exploded and black ooze squirted around him. He yanked hard on the blade, struggling to free it from the metallic sinews and tendons. Venor screeched in fury. The hyperblade came away and flew out of Max's hands. He fell back as the creature's leg buckled. Another leg knocked against him, sending him skidding across the deck.

Max caught a piece of the broken deck

to stop himself sliding into the sea, but the force of the Robobeast's blow jerked the blaster from his other hand. It splashed into the waves.

The scorpion stamped towards him.

I'm facing the toughest Robobeast yet and I've lost all my weapons, Max thought. He stared up at Venor and his chest tightened.

The scorpion arched its tail and struck down at him. Max threw himself aside as the stinger thumped heavily into the deck. Venor roared, trying to pull its tail from the hull, but it was stuck fast in the metal skin of the ship.

This is my last chance, Max realised. He scrambled to his feet, dodging the scorpion's massive claws, and looked around for anything to fight back with. He caught a glimpse of a dull blue glow from the base of the scorpion's stinger. It had to be the

Robobeast's CPU. Siborg had put it on Venor's most dangerous weapon to protect it.

Venor rose up on its claws, screeching and rocking back and forth as it tried to pull its stinger from the deck.

"Max!" Lia shouted. "Use this!"

She hurled the Coral Sword and Max caught it by the hilt.

A great cracking noise filled the air. Venor had pulled its sting free. It narrowed its eyes and reared on its back legs. Its stinger pulsed with green venom. Max's knees weakened.

He adjusted his grip on the sword. A giant claw tried to seize him, but Max dodged it and grabbed on. Suddenly he was jerked into the air. The Robobeast dangled him for a moment, eyes wide, but Max swung off, landing on the scorpion's back. Venor twisted and squirmed, and Max half stumbled, half slid towards the tail.

"Look out!" yelled Lia.

Max saw the stinger descending and swung the Coral Sword by instinct. The blade bit into the beast's tail. Black pus and green venom sprayed across the deck as the stinger crashed to the deck with a sickening thud.

The blue glow was extinguished at once.

Max jumped off to avoid the deadly green goo. Venor spun around to face him again. The Robobeast no longer had its stinger but the creature still had two deadly claws. The scorpion staggered towards Max, its tail stump twitching. Dragging one of its claws, it snapped the other at him. Max ran to the starboard side of the vessel. Venor followed, its weight tilting the ship.

The scorpion slipped. Its legs scrambled frantically against the deck, but it couldn't regain its balance. Max dived out the way as Venor crashed overboard with an enormous splash and vanished beneath the waves.

CHAPTER NINE

A PIRATE LIVES

Max surveyed the damage with a heavy heart. Foul smoke drifted across the deck of the *Lizard's Revenge* from patches of the corrosive venom. Sparks exploded from the ship's damaged systems. Lia was rocking Grace in her arms. The young pirate was sobbing uncontrollably.

She deserves to say a proper goodbye to her uncle, Max realised. *Then we can put a stop to Siborg once and for all.*

Max sent Rivet off the ship to fetch Roger's

body. The dogbot swam through broken pieces of ship and clamped his jaws over Roger's deepsuit, then dragged him, face-up, back to the *Lizard's Revenge*. Max approached the body, hardly able to look. Roger's skin was pale, and his chest was swollen with venom under his black pirate coat. Max sniffed back his tears. He had to be strong for Grace.

He stared down at his friend. He looked so peaceful. "Lia, do you remember when we saved him from the Deadly Rainbow shoal and he pretended to be a research scientist?"

Lia raised her chin, her bottom lip quivering. "He was up to no good, but he nearly always did the right thing in the end."

Grace dropped to her knees beside her uncle's body. She tried to brush his hair with her hand, but her fingers caught on his eye patch and flicked it aside. Roger's other eye looked completely normal!

"Typical Roger," Max said. "Trust him to pretend to have only one good eye!"

Both of Roger's eyes opened and blinked. Max and Lia gasped.

"You're alive!" Grace squealed.

"B… But how?" Lia asked. "We all saw you get stabbed by Venor's sting!"

Roger raised his hand shakily to the top of his deepsuit and unzipped it. Beneath the fabric was the carved stone breastplate of Addulis. He rapped it softly with his knuckles. "I've got a bit of quick thinking to thank for that!"

Max grinned, too relieved that his friend was alive to tease him about his light-fingered ways. "Welcome back to the land of the living!"

As Roger stood up, Grace threw herself at him. "Don't do that again, Uncle!"

Roger laughed, then winced and rubbed his ribs. "It did knock the wind out of my sails. I'll be sorer than a sunburned seagull for a while." He looked around at the twisted and smouldering wreckage of the *Lizard's Revenge*. "Looks like Siborg owes me a new boat. Let's secure these weapons before we make him pay."

Max helped Roger limp across the deck. The

bridge compartment had taken a battering. He pushed open the door. Damage warning lights flashed like an Aquoran disco, but Max knew there was nothing he couldn't fix.

He placed the Coral Sword in the weapons locker along with the Pearl Spear. Roger unclasped the Stone Breastplate and hung it next to them. The ancient battle-gear glowed together. Max's chest swelled with pride. "Just one more object to find and the whole of Nemos will be safe again!"

"You don't think I'm going to allow you to simply walk away with them, do you?" Siborg boomed from the radio.

"We just defeated your Robobeast," Max said. "How are you going to stop us?"

"You're as naive as your mother," Siborg answered. "You've not done anything that I've not wanted you to. Who let you onto my ship and allowed you to escape? Me. I even let you defeat Venor! Did you really believe you did that all on your own? Fools!"

Max bunched up his fists. "If you're such a genius, why have we got three of the Arms of Addulis and not you?"

There was silence over the radio for a moment. "Because you're going to bring them to me, Max," Siborg replied at last, his voice cold.

Max laughed. "And how are you going to make me do that?"

"Perhaps you should take a look at little Grace's ankle," Siborg said.

Max glanced down at Grace's leg. Lia and Grace gasped as they saw it. A wristwatch-sized black box was strapped to Grace's ankle. It had no display screen, face, or buttons, except for a small flashing red light and a stubby antenna.

"Stuffed octopus, what have you done to

my niece?" Roger snapped.

"I'd have thought that was obvious," Siborg replied. "It's a bomb."

Grace tugged at it. "Get it off me! I don't want to lose a leg."

Siborg snorted. "Don't be silly. It may be small like you but that device has enough high-powered explosives to blow up the entire ship."

Max wiped the sweat from his hands and knelt down to study the ankle bomb. *There has to be a way to disarm it*, he thought.

"And I don't recommend attempting to remove it," Siborg added. "Any form of tampering will set it off. I'll leave the door open for you, Max. Come alone, and don't forget to bring the Arms of Addulis."

With a blast of static, Siborg's voice went silent.

Roger's face burned red as he hugged Grace. "If I get my hands on him I'll feed him to the sharks!"

"How did he put it there?" Lia asked. "Grace was with us the whole time."

Max kicked a broken piece of control panel. He couldn't believe they'd been outmanoeuvred, again. "It must have happened after we escaped the lab-ship and the cyrate grabbed Grace in the water."

Even that was just a ruse. He's been toying with us at every step!

Max steadied his breath as he located a handheld scanner. He examined the device on Grace's ankle, then threw the scanner aside. "I can't even get a reading," he cursed. "It's too high-tech."

Grace began to cry again. "I'm sorry."

Max gripped her shoulder. He could feel heat rising inside him. "It's not your fault. It's Siborg's!"

"What are you going to do?" Lia asked, her face pale with fear.

"The only thing I can do," Max replied, gritting his teeth. "I'm going to take the weapons to Siborg."

CHAPTER TEN

NEW TRICKS

With the ancient weapons strapped in next to him, Max gunned his hydrodisk towards Siborg's lab-ship. Lia raced alongside him on Spike, Rivet swimming nearby.

"You can't trust Siborg," she said. "He'll trick you."

"I know that, Lia," Max told her. "But if I don't go alone, Grace's life is in danger."

"Come with Max," the dogbot barked.

Max shook his head. "No, Riv. Not this time. Stay with Lia, do what she says," he ordered, trying not let his voice choke. "She'll look after you."

"Come, Rivet," Lia said as she and Spike swam away.

The dogbot's tail slipped between his legs as he followed them. Max took a deep breath and pushed the throttle forward.

As the hydrodisk approached the *Hive*, a cargo door slid open. Max surged inside. He surfaced in the submersible pool of a large loading bay. Crates were stacked around the outer walls and crab-like pincers hung from the ceiling.

Max scanned the bay and registered a sign of life behind a wall of crates. The shield dome on the hydrodisk retracted and Max reached for his hyperblade.

"You won't need that!" Siborg's voice boomed.

Siborg stalked around the crates in his

battle suit. The hand they'd damaged in the holding bay was already repaired, and the blasters and rocket launchers along its arms and legs whirled into action. Red targeting lasers sprouted from the suit. Max glanced at his chest and felt his blood go cold. Every one of Siborg's weapons was aimed at him.

"Bring out the Arms of Addulis so I can see them," Siborg demanded.

Max unstrapped the ancient Merryn weapons and climbed out. He stared at the viewing panel in the battle suit's chest, but it was impossible to see through the polarised glass. *Why doesn't he show himself?* Max wondered.

"Come out and take them yourself!" he said.

"I'm content to conduct business from this suit." Siborg raised an arm and picked up a black stick topped with two glowing buttons. "Now, lay down the Arms of Addulis and leave before I decide to blow up your friends."

That must be the detonator! Max realised. He felt his throat tighten. If he got this wrong, his friends would die. "What guarantee do I have that once you have the weapons, you won't still blow us up anyway?"

"You have my word," Siborg replied.

"Forgive me," Max said, "but your word isn't enough."

Siborg sighed. "You're in no position to bargain. However, if you give me the weapons I'll let you have the detonator. If you press the green button, it will release your friend."

Max nodded. *He's right – I have no choice here.* He placed the weapons on the deck and stepped back.

Siborg's battle suit stamped nearer to the Arms of Addulis.

Max kept his weight on the balls of his feet in case he needed to run forward and grab the weapons. "Now give me the detonator."

"Catch," Siborg said. He threw the detonator.

Max heart raced. He sprinted after the detonator as it arced through the air. Max dived at full stretch and caught the stick just before it hit the floor.

Max breathed a sigh of relief, and looked

up to see Siborg slinging the Merryn weapons over his shoulder. "Because you've been so kind," Siborg said, "you can have ten seconds to leave the ship."

Hatches opened across the ceilings and cyrates dropped down into the loading bay. They landed in a crouch with their blasters already trained on Max. As they straightened,

Max's chest tightened. He sprinted to the hydrodisk with the detonator and leapt into the control seat. He activated the dome and it slid into place.

Blaster fire hit the hydrodisk. Max gripped the nav-wheel and pushed his engines into full reverse. He shot out of the lab-ship backwards and spun around so he could see where he was going.

"One last thing about the detonator…" Siborg's voice came through from the communications panel. Something squirmed in Max's stomach. "It's fake. So is the bomb. I'm not an animal, you know."

Max slammed his fist against the nav-wheel. He'd been tricked by Siborg again. He'd given away the ancient weapons for nothing. He felt sick. *Siborg's too clever*, he thought.

He steered towards the *Lizard's Revenge*. There were holes across the deck and hull where Venor had ripped away the panelling. Smoke was still drifting from the stern and a pair of gun turrets dangled off the front of the ship.

Max sailed the hydrodisk into the storage bay and found Roger knee deep in spare engine parts. Lia and Grace were trying to move replacement panelling with the robotic hoist system. They left the panels hanging and ran to him.

Max opened the plexiglass dome.

"Is my Grace safe?" Roger asked.

Max picked up the detonator and threw it at the wall. As it shattered in little black pieces, Lia and Grace gasped. "The explosives weren't even real," Max said. He bent down and cut the narrow black band off Grace's ankle. "It was just a trick," he yelled, throwing it out of the cargo bay doors.

The scanners showed Siborg's vessel vanish

under the waves. Perhaps if they followed him straight away, they might win the weapons back. "How are the engines?" he asked.

"See for yourself," Roger replied.

Max climbed from the cargo hold to the bridge. Almost every system of the ship had flashing warning lights. Roger sucked air between his teeth.

Max studied the control screens. "It's not all bad," he said. "Weapons are down, but if we re-route power from those systems and make some adjustments, I can get the engines back up to seventy per cent power. But Siborg will be long gone before I'm finished."

"That's where it's your turn to thank me!" Lia said, pointing to the nav station. A large red blip was heading across a map of the Chaos Quadrant. "That's Siborg's ship. While I was waiting for you, I put a tracker on it."

Max scratched his head. "Did I just hear

you right? You – using technology?"

Lia raised her eyebrows. "Take a look through the seascope."

Max peered down the seascope that was tracking Siborg's ship. *What is she using as a tracker?* he wondered.

He increased the magnification and saw Rivet clamped like a limpet to Siborg's ship. Max laughed at the sight. "You'll be building

your own aquabike next!"

Lia shook her head. "You don't really think that is ever going to happen, do you?"

Grace pulled at Max's arm. "Next time I see Siborg, he won't know what hit him!" She waved her plastic blaster towards the radar screen.

"He's going to answer to all of us, or I'm no pirate," Roger said. "Time we got the *Lizard's Revenge* ready for our next fight."

Max grinned. Siborg hadn't counted on the loyalty of his friends or their determination to put a stop to his evil plans. Next time, Max and the gang would be ready for him – and nothing would stop them recovering all of the precious Merryn treasures!

Don't miss Max's next Sea Quest adventure,
when he faces

MONOTH
THE SPIKED
DESTROYER

WIN AN EXCLUSIVE GOODY BAG

In every Sea Quest book the Sea Quest logo is hidden in one of the pictures. Find the logos in books 17-20, make a note of which pages they appear on and go online to enter the competition at

www.seaquestbooks.co.uk

Each month we will put all of the correct entries into a draw and select one winner to receive a special Sea Quest goody bag.

You can also send your entry on a postcard to:

Sea Quest Competition, Orchard Books, 338 Euston Road, London, NW1 3BH

Don't forget to include your name and address!

GOOD LUCK

Closing Date: 30th April 2015

IF YOU LIKE SEA QUEST, YOU'LL LOVE BEAST QUEST!

Series 1: COLLECT THEM ALL!

An evil wizard has enchanted the magical beasts of Avantia. Only a true hero can free the beasts and save the land. Is Tom the hero Avantia has been waiting for?

978 1 84616 483 5

978 1 84616 482 8

978 1 84616 484 2

978 1 84616 486 6

978 1 84616 485 9

978 1 84616 487 3

DON'T MISS THE
BRAND NEW SERIES OF:

Series 15: VELMAL'S REVENGE

978 1 40833 487 4

978 1 40833 489 8

978 1 40833 491 1

978 1 40833 493 5

COMING SOON